Celebrating

Veronica

by Suzanne Marshall

LiveWellMedia.com

ISBN: 9798626567366

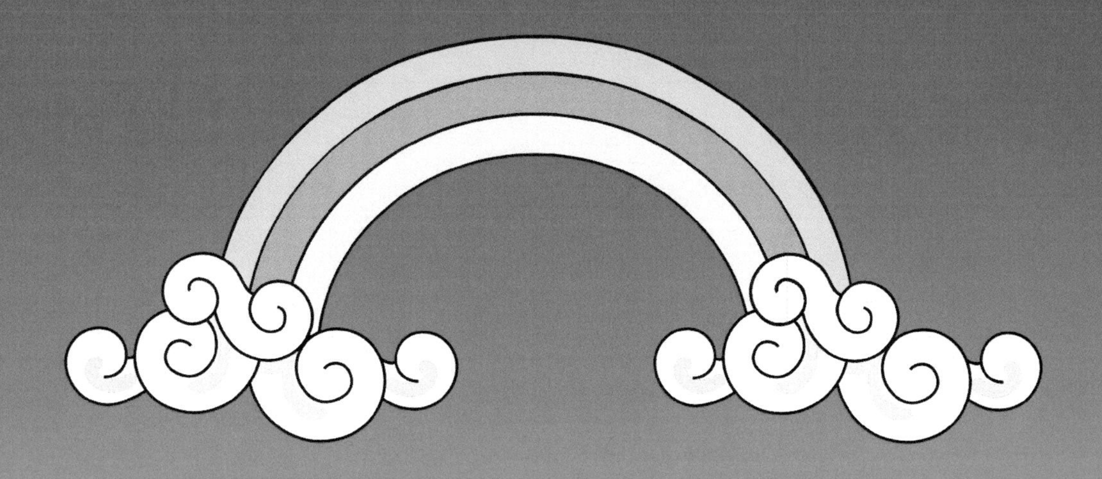

This book is dedicated to

Veronica

who is loved very much!

Veronica,

on the day you were born,
the stars above
glowed with joy
and twinkled with love.

Just ahead, Veronica,
great adventures await...

You'll explore and discover.
You'll dream and create.

You'll find fun friends, Veronica.
You'll have a hoot.

You'll go places
exciting and new!

You'll learn all about you
and the whole world too.

Along the way, Veronica,
there will be some boo-boos,
but throughout it all,
I'll be here for you.

Everybody babbles
before they talk.

Everybody wobbles
before they walk.

You'll grow stronger,
Veronica,
and braver too,
as you realize
all you can do.

You'll come to see,
Veronica,
believe it or not:
all you need
you've already got.

You've got love, Veronica, right inside you.
It's yours to share and spread around you.

You've got smiles,
Veronica,
and playfulness
to fill your life
with happiness.

I'm cheering you on,
Veronica,
as you grow
with a "Yay!"
and "Hooray!"
and a big "Bravo!"

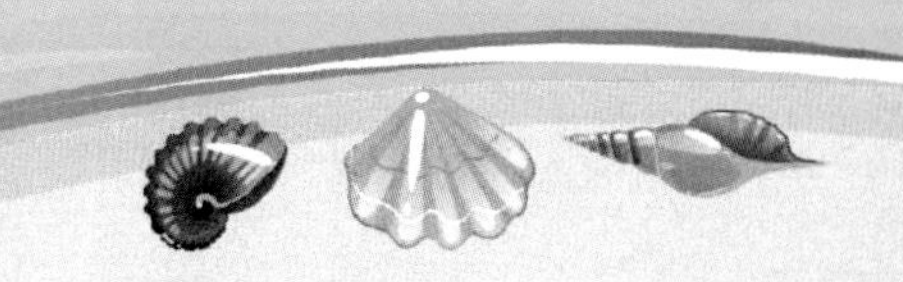

Veronica,
here's a little secret
I'll share with you...
I can't wait to see
all the fun things
you'll do!

You're adorable, Veronica.
You sparkle and shine.

You're very special; one of a kind.

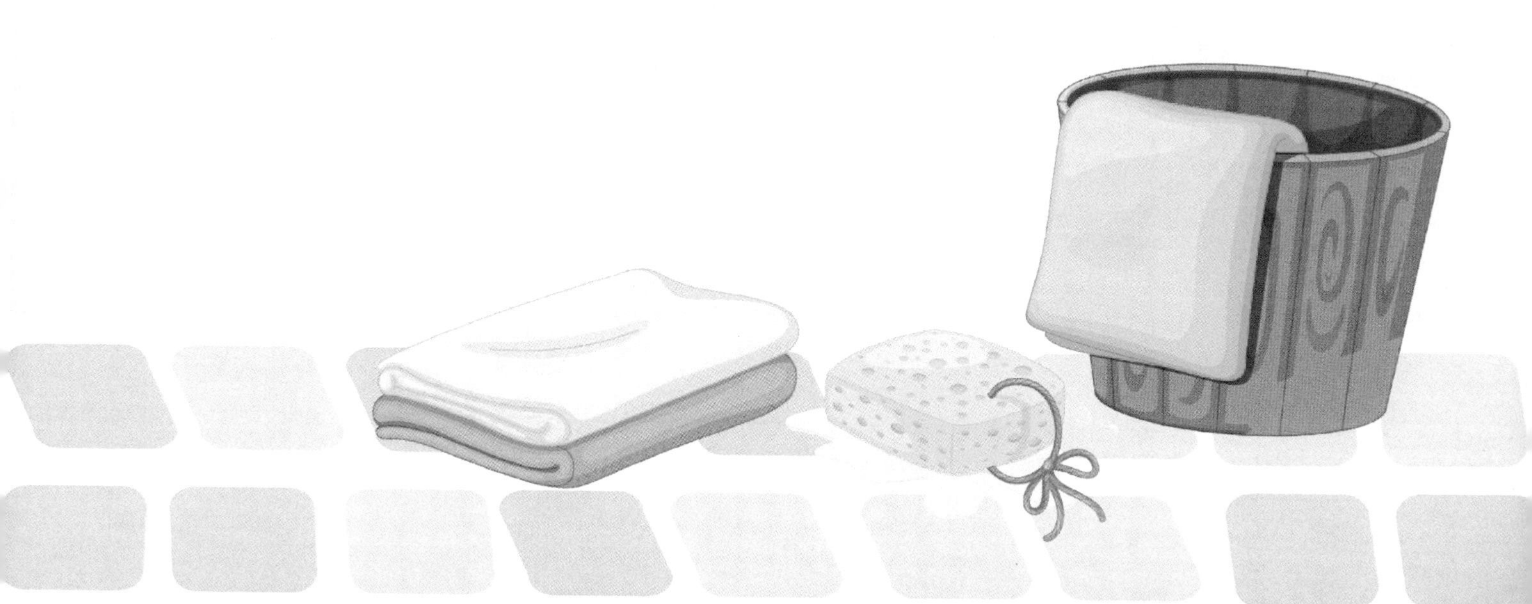

I love you, Veronica,
more than I can say.

I love you more
each and every day.

Special Thanks

to my mom and dad for their ongoing love and support, and to my awesome editorial team: Rachel and Hannah Roeder, and Don Marshall. Illustrations have been edited by the author. Most background images were curated from freepik.com and freedesignfile.com. Credits include bunny: © iaRada; globe, school, house: ©AlexBannykh; bathtub/bathroom: © lovesiyu; toucan with animals, islands, bath items: © colematt; bugs/insects: © colematt and clairev.

About the Author

Suzanne Marshall writes to inspire, engage and empower children. Her books are full of positive affirmations and inspirational quotes. An honors graduate of Smith College, Suzanne has been a prize-winning videographer and produced playwright. Learn more about her personalized books at: **LiveWellMedia.com**.
(Pictured below: Suzanne Marshall and her rescue dog Abby Underdog)

Made in the USA
Las Vegas, NV
20 October 2022